This book belongs to:

_____

For Isabel

This paperback edition first published in 2013 by Andersen Press Ltd.

First published in Great Britain in 1994 by Andersen Press Ltd.,

20 Vauxhall Bridge Road, London SW1V 2SA.

Published in Australia by Random House Australia Pty.,

Level 3, 100 Pacific Highway, North Sydney, NSW 2060.

Copyright © David McKee, 1994.

The rights of David McKee to be identified as the author and illustrator

of this work have been asserted by him in accordance with the

Copyright, Designs and Patents Act, 1988.

All rights reserved.

Colour separated in Switzerland by Photolitho AG, Zürich.

Printed and bound in Singapore by Tien Wah Press.

10   9   8   7   6   5   4   3   2   1

British Library Cataloguing in Publication Data available.

ISBN 978 1 84939 689 9

Isabel's NOISY Tummy

David McKee

Andersen Press

Isabel was a very good girl.
She was helpful and she always did as she was told.
But, Isabel had a noisy tummy.

At school her tummy burbled. The children giggled.
"Was that you, Isabel?" said the teacher.
"No, Miss, that was my tummy," replied Isabel.

"You eat too quickly, Isabel," said her mother.
"No wonder you have a noisy tummy."
Isabel ate more slowly.

At school her tummy burbled and rumbled.

"He, he, he," the children sniggered.

"Isabel, was that you?" asked the teacher.

"No, Miss, that was my tummy," said Isabel.

"You don't get enough exercise, Isabel," said her father.
"No wonder you have a noisy tummy."
Isabel got up early and ran three times around the park.
Then she ate her breakfast very slowly.

At school Isabel's tummy burbled and rumbled and gurgled.

"Ha, ha, ha," laughed the children.

"Isabel, was that you?" sighed the teacher.

"No, Miss, that was my tummy," said Isabel.

Isabel's mother took her to the doctor. "Take a spoonful of this first thing in the morning," he said.
In the morning, Isabel took a spoonful of medicine. It tasted awful. Then she ran four times around the park and afterwards slowly ate her breakfast.

At school her tummy burbled and rumbled and gurgled and mumbled.

"Ho, ho, ho," guffawed the children.

"Isabel, was that you?" snapped the teacher.

"No, Miss, that was my tummy," said Isabel.

That day the teacher took the class to the zoo.
They saw the crocodiles.

They visited the monkey house.

They saw the hippo take a bath.

And the elephant take a shower.

When they arrived at the tiger it was feeding time. The keeper
opened the gate to pass in the food, and then he slipped.

The hungry tiger leapt forward, looked at the children and roared.

The children shook with fear.

The teacher panicked.

Somebody screamed.

Isabel's tummy roared.

It roared even louder than the tiger.

The tiger backed away in surprise.

The keeper jumped up, passed in the food and closed the door.

"Was that you?" the keeper asked Isabel.

"No, Sir, that was my tummy," said Isabel.

The children cheered. The teacher smiled with relief.

The next day when Isabel arrived at school
the children stood and clapped.

All that day the children waited, but Isabel's tummy stayed quiet.

"It's probably tired after such a huge roar," the children agreed.

It was the same the next day, and the next. The children sighed in disappointment. But by the end of the week they had forgotten all about Isabel's tummy.

Then, suddenly, there was a loud noise.
The children collapsed with laughter.

The teacher turned and smiled.

"Isabel," she said, "was that your tummy?"

"No, Miss," said Isabel. "That was my bottom."

Other books by
David McKee

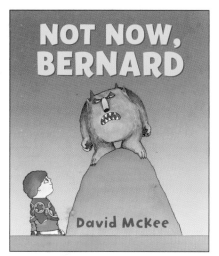

9781849394673

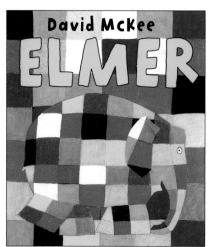

9781842707319

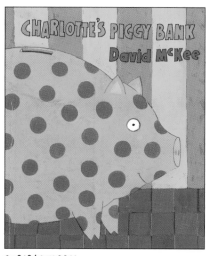

9781842703311

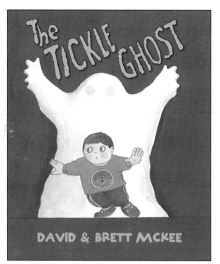

9781849392907

9781842704684

9781849393898